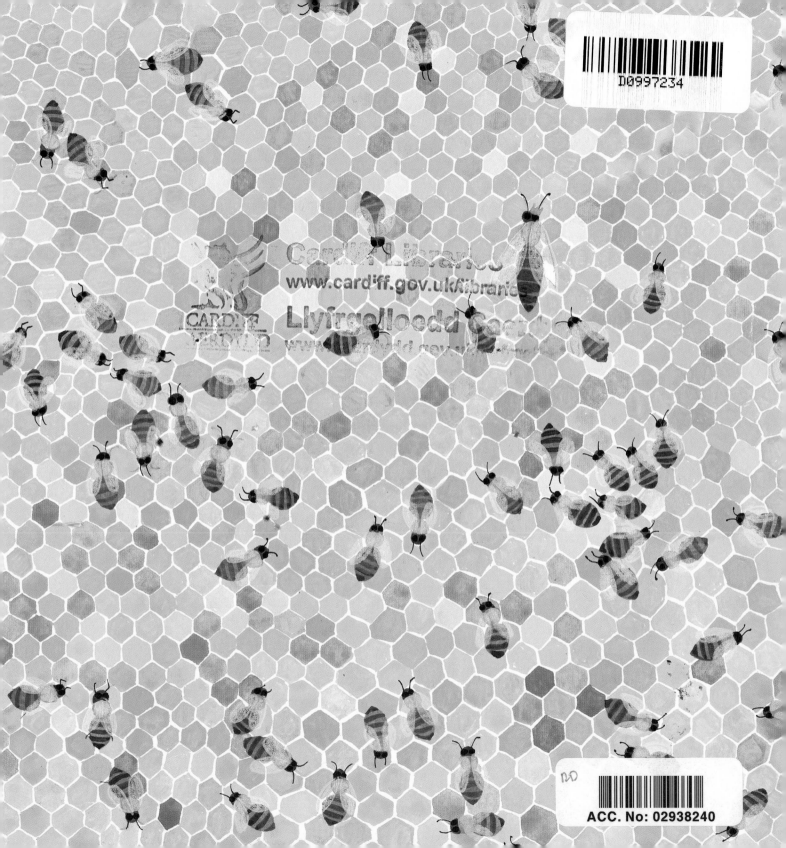

Little Honey Bee

*C.L.: To Gwenno, my little honey bee,
and in memory of two lovely grandmothers.
V.L.: To my grandmother, Mamie Léone.*

First impression: 2018

© Caryl Lewis & Y Lolfa Cyf., 2018
© Illustrations copyright Valériane Leblond

This book is subject to copyright and may not be reproduced by any means except for review purposes without the prior written consent of the publishers.

The publishers wish to acknowledge the support of Cyngor Llyfrau Cymru.

ISBN: 978-1-78461-561-1

Published and printed in Wales on paper from well-maintained forests by Y Lolfa Cyf., Talybont, Ceredigion SY24 5HE
e-mail ylolfa@ylolfa.com
website www.ylolfa.com
tel 01970 832 304
fax 832 782

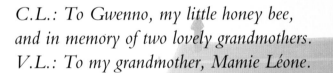

Little Honey Bee

Caryl Lewis

Illustrated by Valériane Leblond

y Lolfa

Elsi hadn't spoken since being left on her grandmother's doorstep in the darkest hours of the night. Her grandmother had wrapped her in a colourful blanket and carried her to the chair in front of the fire before warming some milk on the stove.

A week had passed since then, but the only thing Elsi did was stare out of the whitewashed cottage, silent as snow.

The hedgehogs were busy curling into prickly balls.

The songbirds were begging for crumbs.

And the squirrels were seeking their hidden stashes of nuts.

Usually, Elsi would have run outside to play in the silvery softness, but her heart was heavy and her tongue was even heavier.

"It's nice to be quiet sometimes," her grandmother said whilst brushing Elsi's golden hair by firelight. "Think of winter. Winter's always quiet. The earth resting. Gathering strength for when the spring comes…"

8

One morning, Grandma placed a creamy bowl of porridge in front of Elsi. Then she reached for a small pot of honey from the dresser, before slipping her hand into her apron pocket and taking out a special spoon decorated with a golden honey bee. Very carefully, she drizzled the honey onto the porridge in the shape of a curly 'E'. Elsi ate in silence as the taste of summer flowers bloomed on her tongue. She smiled.

Outside, the world was beginning to thaw.

Early one morning, as spring was pushing the first flowers into the startling sunshine, Grandma came to Elsi's room and whispered gently into her ear. "Come with me, my little honey bee…"

Elsi followed her down the winding path to the bottom of the garden, where she saw the most astonishing sight she had ever seen!

At the bottom of the garden was a village!
A tiny little village.
A pretty little house with a golden bell on its roof.
A little house with a blue door and windows.
A church with colourful windows and a white cottage
with flowers at its door.

Elsi looked at Grandma in surprise.
"I wonder if anyone's at home?" Grandma said, with
a mischievous smile that Elsi was beginning to love.
Grandma pressed her ear to one little house and
listened for a sign that someone was in. Elsi leant
closer too.

B zzzzzzzzzzzzzzzzzzzzzzzzzzzzzzzzzzzzzzzzzzzzzzzzzzzzzzzzzzzz...

"Bees!" exclaimed Elsi.

As her first word in weeks left her mouth, Elsi felt a quivering deep down inside her.

"A whole village of bees," Grandma nodded.

Grandma threw a veil around her head and arranged one around Elsi too. She opened the roof of the little house and showed Elsi the queen bee.

"Oh, I can see her crown!" said Elsi. Grandma smiled at her.

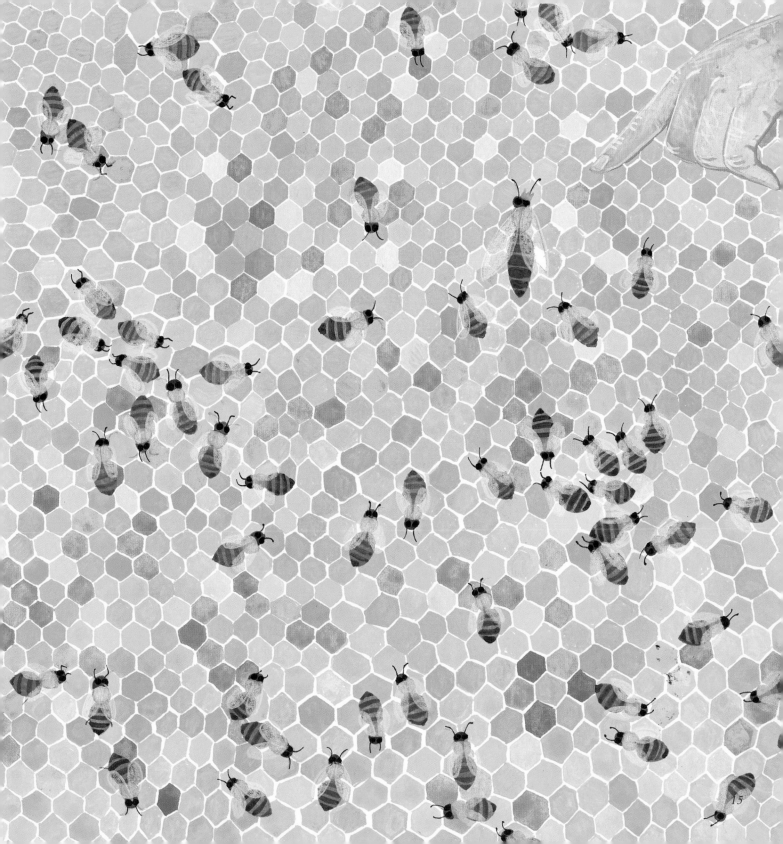

Elsi watched as spring touched the garden in a thousand little ways. She followed the bees to the bluebells and heard the flowers tinkling as the bees brushed by. She followed them from one flower to the next.

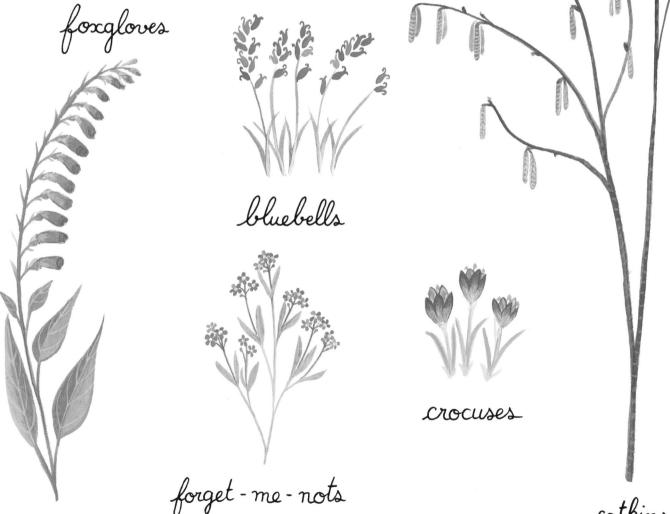

foxgloves

bluebells

forget-me-nots

crocuses

catkins

rosemary

heather

lavender

clover

And as she followed them, she came to know every secret place in the garden and to learn every flower's name. She tasted their perfect names with her mouth, rolling the letters around with her tongue.

Elsi forgot about her silence and she started to talk and sing and hum with the bees.

In summer, Elsi and Grandma would eat at a little table under the apple tree, the air around them busy with bees.

By watching them, Elsi noticed that they would dance in order to talk to each other. By wiggling their bottoms back and forth, they'd tell each other where the best flowers were.

Elsi would dance too.

And wiggle her bottom.

And her grandmother would laugh and laugh.

lsi also noticed that the bees would fall in love with one special kind of flower and would visit them time after time after time…

Then they carried the pollen back to the hive on their legs.

Elsi would laugh as they bumbled their way back, heavy with pollen, like someone carrying too many shopping bags.

Sometimes, if big, glassy drops of rain were falling heavily in the garden, the bees weren't able to fly. Elsi would sit on the window sill and wait for the clouds to pass.

And when she wasn't following the bees, she would plant flowers for them in the old garden until the little patch was full to the brim with colour and light and scent.

Grandma would watch her, smiling.

Early one morning, Elsi heard a tinkling in the kitchen. She pulled on her dress and ran down the narrow stairs. Grandma was lining up jars on the kitchen table. Her veil was already around her head.

She smiled…

"Summer is fading," she said. "So, the time has come…"

Elsi placed her veil over her own head and followed
Grandma to the little village at the bottom of the garden.
There, Grandma opened the hives, letting
their sweet, spicy scent perfume the
air around them. She pulled
frame after frame,
heavy with
honey, from
the little houses,
making sure she
left the bees
enough food
to last them
through the
winter.

In the kitchen, Grandma scraped the honey from the frames into a bowl before wrapping the honeycombs in a light muslin cloth and hanging it up. The table and the floor, and Elsi, were covered in sticky honey. Afterwards, Grandma and Elsi had a cup of tea whilst watching the rest of the golden honey drip luxuriously into the clean jars.

Autumn arrived, and the bees were preparing to sleep for the winter.

The flowers were closing their petals.
The squirrels were stashing away shiny new nuts.
The hedgehogs were looking for cosy nests.
The conkers were swelling beautifully in their spiky skins.
And leaves as large as Elsi's hands were weaving their
way down from the treetops.
"Well," sighed Grandma, "that's summer over for
another year…" but Elsi didn't hear her.
She was fast asleep in Grandma's lap.

When winter came round once again, Elsi wasn't sad.
She would make paper crowns like the queen bee's and
decorate them with gold.
She would fly like a bee around the garden.

She would recite the names of the flowers.
She would name all the colours in her world.
She would dream of the bees and their humming
would fill her dreams.
And best of all, every now and then she would be
allowed to go to the pantry to fetch a new pot of
honey. Grandma would use her special spoon to drizzle
it on her porridge and make a curly E before leaning
over to whisper in her ear…

Elsi grew into a beautiful woman, with silky hair the colour of honey. She had a daughter of her own and brought her up by herself in the cottage with the tiny village at the bottom of the garden. And even though life was not always easy, Grandma's words always hummed in her head…

"Remember, even when winter is at its coldest, summer will always come round again…"

y Lolfa

www.ylolfa.com

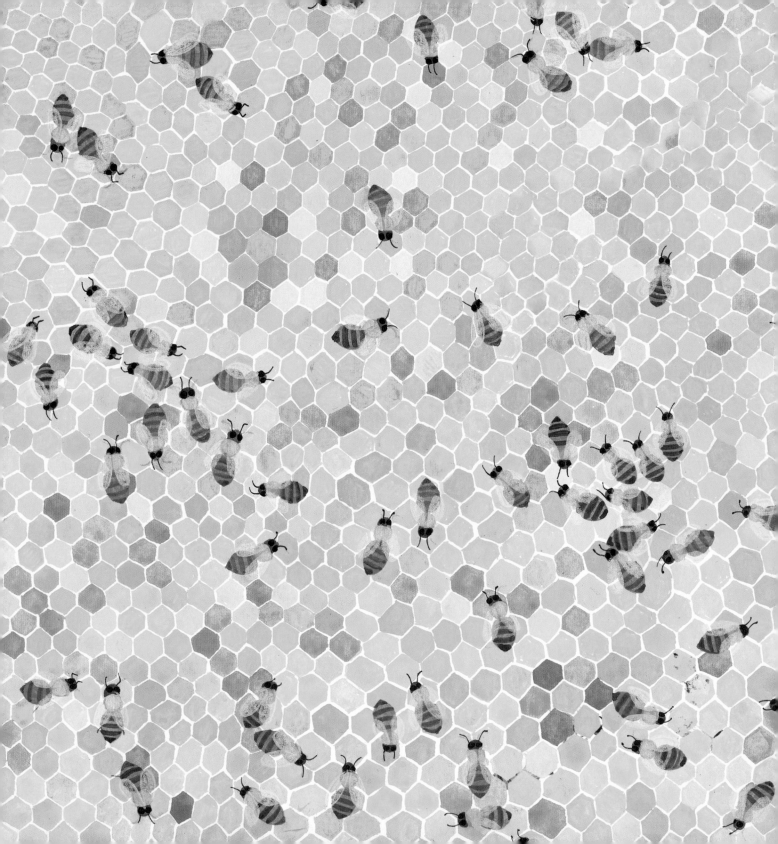